For Mommy Bears everywhere ~ A. R.

For Jenny, the best big sister in the world,
and for our mom ~ A. E.

This edition published for Scholastic Inc., 557 Broadway; New York, NY 10012,
by arrangement with Little Tiger Press.
SCHOLASTIC and associated logos are trademarks and/or registered trademarks
of Scholastic Inc. Scholastic Canada Ltd.; Markham, Ontario

First published in the United States by Good Books, Intercourse, PA 17534, 2009

Library of Congress Cataloging-in-Publication Data is available for this title

Original edition published in English by Little Tiger Press,
an imprint of Magi Publications, London, England, 2009.

Text copyright © Alison Ritchie 2009
Illustrations copyright © Alison Edgson 2009

ISBN 13: 978-1-84506-944-5
ISBN 10: 1-84506-944-7

Printed in China

2 4 6 8 10 9 7 5 3 1

Me and My Mom!

Alison Ritchie

illustrated by Alison Edgson

Me and my mom
are together all day.
I follow her footsteps
as we go out to play.

We make strings of flowers,
and Mom is so clever
That *her* daisy chain
seems to go on forever!

We roar in the cave,
and it answers our call
With magical echoes—
one big and one small.

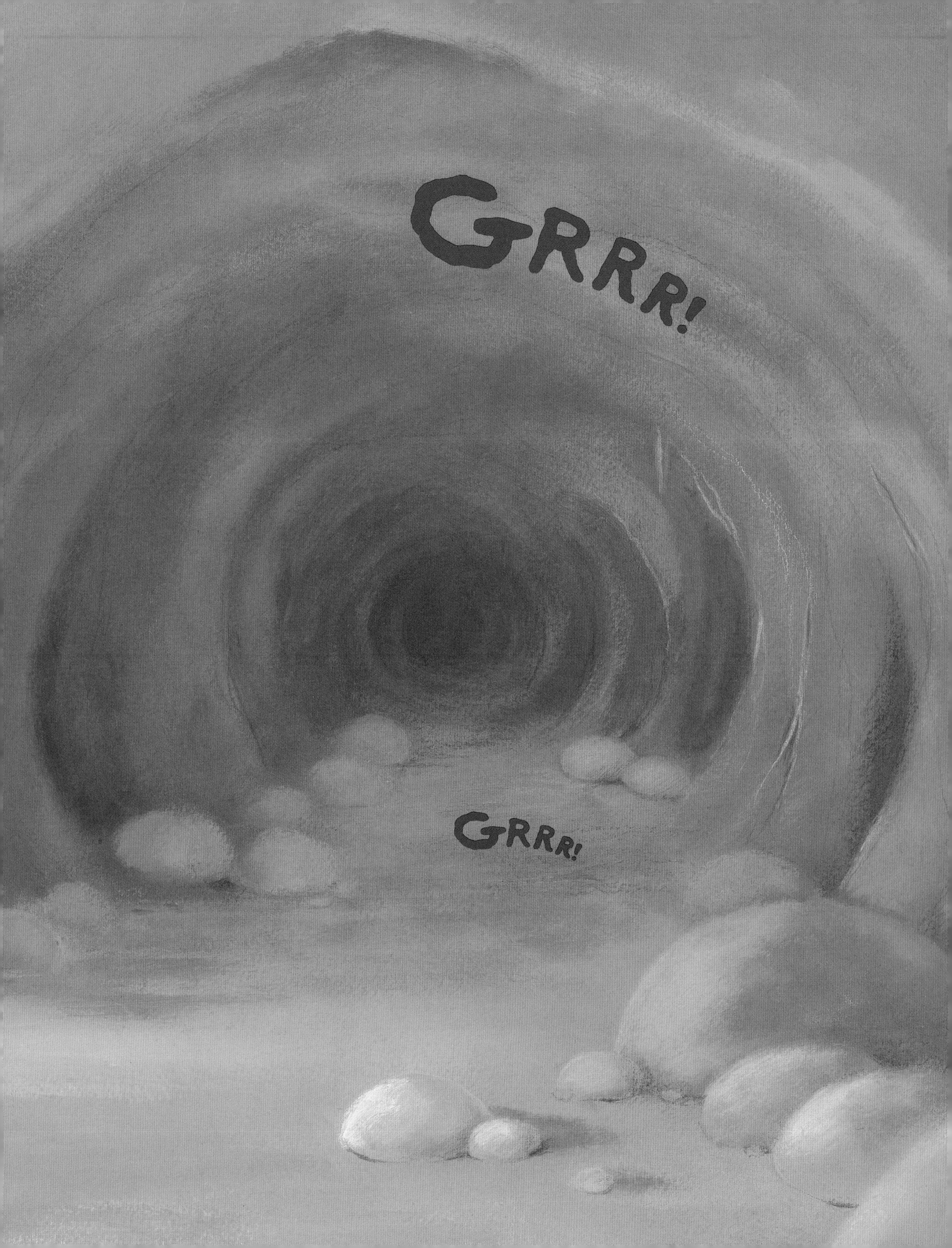
GRRR!
GRRR!

My mom's not afraid
of the dark or the night.
And I'm brave like her
when she's holding me tight!

We know a good trick,
my mommy and me—
I balance one apple,
and Mom can do three!

The ice is so slippery,
it's easy to fall.
But soon, just like Mom,
I won't tumble at all!

We glide through the water,
and I make a wish
That one day, like Mom,
I will swim like a fish!

With a showery spray,
my mom dries her fur.
I wiggle my bottom
and shake just like her.

It's a long way to jump—
I'm not sure if I dare.
But I know I'll be safe
with my mommy right there!

We scoop up some leaves
and throw them up high,
Then watch as they float
gently down from the sky.

From my soft, furry ears
to the tips of my toes,
Mom says I'm the best little
bear cub she knows!

My mommy is special
in every way.
I want to be just like
my mommy someday.